FIVE GET GRAN ONLINE

Other adventures in this series:

Enid Blyton

FIVE GET GRAN ONLINE

Text by
Bruno Vincent

Enid Blyton for Grown-Ups

Quercus

First published in Great Britain in 2017 by

Quercus Editions Ltd
Carmelite House
50 Victoria Embankment
London EC4Y 0DZ

An Hachette UK company

A CIP catalogue record for this book is available
from the British Library

ISBN 978 1 78648 386 7

Text by Bruno Vincent
Original illustrations by Eileen A. Soper
Cover illustration by Ruth Palmer

10 9 8 7 6

Typeset by CC Book Production

Printed and bound in Great Britain by Clays Ltd, Elcograf S.p.A

Contents

CHAPTER ONE

Five Get Cyber-security Conscious

It had been a long, harrowing year of fake news, online abuse, misogynist doxing, ransomware attacks and state-sponsored cyber terrorism. Like many others, Julian, Anne, George and Dick felt the world was becoming a colder and harsher place, for no reason that they could really understand or control.

The devices that ordinary people relied upon to live their lives were being turned into weapons against them and, one morning in early autumn, Anne, Dick and George found themselves sitting at the kitchen table being subjected to yet another lecture from Julian.

'It's all about security!' he said for the third time.

Anne was painting her nails and George was reading a piece about Gamergate on her phone, while Dick flicked through Anne's discarded *Stylist* magazine with a look of profound mystification.

'You never know when they'll get you!' Julian went on.

'We must be vigilant! At all times! So I hope you've updated your software protection.'

'No point,' said Anne. 'If they want to get you, they'll get you.'

'What do you mean?' asked Julian. 'Also, what's this ice cream doing out of the freezer?'

'It's not ice cream,' said George, 'it's Bolognese. Look at the writing on the top.'

'Actually, that writing's out of date,' said Anne. 'It's really rhubarb crumble in there. I don't know why it's out of the freezer, though.'

'Oh, sorry,' said Dick. 'It won't fit any more. Had to make room for my laptop.'

They all stopped what they were doing and looked at him.

'It's the new thing,' he said. 'I read somewhere if you really don't want your computer to get hacked—'

'Oh, don't be ridiculous,' said Julian. 'We don't have to be that paranoid.'

'Haven't you been reading the paper?' George asked. 'Almost any household item is at risk, these days. They can activate your phone, even if it's not on. The C.I.A. can use your coffee machine to spy on you.'

*It had been a long, harrowing year of fake news,
online abuse, misogynist doxing, ransomware attacks
and state-sponsored cyber terrorism.*

'Well, I'm glad it's good for something,' said Julian. 'It certainly doesn't make coffee.'

But George had touched a nerve. Julian put his lecture on hold for the moment and sat down to do some research. Within minutes, he was saucer-eyed with paranoia.

'I had no idea it was *this bad*,' he said, jumping up. 'It's outrage! A gross intrusion! A breach of my fundamental human rights!'

The others had already returned to painting their nails and reading.

'Right,' said Julian. 'There's nothing else for it. I'm going to live in the Australian outback.'

'Don't be stupid,' said Anne. 'You can't afford the plane fare.'

'And they have spiders the size of your face,' said George. 'You hate spiders.'

'Fine.' Julian marched to his room and emerged fifteen minutes later in hiking boots and with a waterproof zipped up to his nose. On his back was a rucksack bulging with his possessions.

'I can't stand this oppression,' said his muffled voice. 'I'm leaving. I'll head north and make a new life for myself in the wilds of the Lake District. Or the Peak District. If they're not the same thing. What *is* that noise?'

'That's the stupid text-alert on your new phone,' George said. 'I've told you to change it.'

'Oh,' said Julian. Dumping his rucksack on the floor and peeling the waterproof hood back from his scalp, he sat to look at it. 'It's another of those weird texts I keep getting,' he said, putting his phone aside. 'There've been half a dozen, now, from the same number. They're freaking me out.'

'I've been getting those as well,' said Anne, blowing on her nails. 'They're so annoying. I assume they're from some scammer – all in broken English, of course.'

'Me too,' said Dick. 'Isn't it odd?'

'Usually, I try to mess with them,' said Julian. 'I reply something like, "Please tell me more about your exciting Viagra offer and I will send bank details".'

'Wait a minute, wait a minute,' said George. 'What are you all talking about?'

'Spam texts,' said Anne. 'Don't you get them?'

'Of course I don't,' George said. 'There's no such thing. Can I see?'

Anne showed hers, and so did Dick.

'But these are from the same number,' said George, looking from one phone to the other, mystified. Checking Julian's phone, she found his were from the same number too. 'Listen to this.' George read aloud: '"How mch c you miss u will see when LOVE". And how about this, from Dick's phone: "Love much underetand not maek it but beEFORr crsms???"'

'Gibberish,' said Julian, 'plain and simple.'

'Pay attention, Julian,' said George testily. 'It's the same person trying to contact all three of you! If it was a scammer, the numbers would be different. It *can't* be coincidence. For instance: this, from your phone, Julian: "Many retns PRESENT coming see me." This is ringing a bell,' George said ominously, and, rather than speculate about it any further, she typed the number into her phone to see if it was recognized, and instinctively pressed *Dial*. 'Oh my goodness,' she said, as they heard the burr of the ringing tone at the other end. 'Why didn't I think of her?'

'Who?' asked Dick.

'Yes, who?' said Julian. 'Tell us, for Pete's sake!'

'Hello?' said a tiny voice from the phone. 'Hello? I can't hear – who is this? Is anyone there?'

'Hi, Granny B!' said George, putting the phone to her ear.

FIVE GET CYBER-SECURITY CONSCIOUS

The others, looking at each other, gasped in joint shock and wonderment. It had been more than twenty years since they had seen or heard from her. Granny B! They'd managed to forget a whole grandparent!

CHAPTER TWO

Catching the Train North

There were mitigating circumstances in the young cousins' forgetfulness. Soon after Julian, Anne and Dick's grandfather had passed away, nearly twenty years ago now, Granny Barnard had married again, and after that, with a new family to get to know and a bevy of new grandchildren, she had been a marked absence from Kirrin family gatherings. And it wasn't for the want of invitations. She was rigorously invited to every get-together that could conceivably include her, but she hated to travel and always politely declined. By a slow and gradual process, they (and she, it was felt) had begun to get used to her not being around.

'So she's not your gran, then, George?' Dick asked, as the train chugged north out of King's Cross.

'No,' George said. 'I'm just along for the ride. I've told work my grandma's sick, so if we could get a couple of shots of her looking pasty, that would be ideal. It's not that much of a lie – I've always thought of Granny B as my grandmother too. I guess she's pretty doddery now.'

'Oh, I'm sure she's *smashing*,' said Anne. Then she looked out of the window at the north London suburbs as they flashed by, and reflected how often she said things that she didn't really mean at all.

'So, listen,' said Julian, plonking himself back down in his seat, having made an early raid on the buffet car (or 'on-board shop' as it prosaically insisted on calling itself). He had a four-pack of cider and a one-volume edition of Evelyn Waugh's *Sword of Honour* trilogy to work through, and was giddy with anticipation. 'One big question: what do we call her?'

'What?' asked George.

'Exactly,' Julian said. 'What? I mean, we haven't seen her since we were all little. I know we always referred to her as Granny B, but she's remarried since then. More than once, if memory serves. Didn't we used to have one of those infantile nicknames for her? You know, like all grandparents get from toddlers – Ga-Ga, or Boo-Boo, or Nang-Nang.'

'People don't let those survive into adulthood,' said George. 'Do they? No? Ugh.'

'Hang on,' said Dick. 'Let's start with the basics. What's her actual name?'

There was a silence around the table.

'I hadn't thought of that,' said Julian. 'I suppose Mummy would be offended if I texted her to ask?'

'Oh, come on,' said Anne. 'You can't possibly not know her name?'

'Why should I know it more than you?' asked Julian. 'We were all under seven the last time we saw her. And what child ever addresses a grandparent by their first name?'

Dick was staring into space, contemplatively tapping his chin. 'I'm sure I knew it once, but I'm stump— *Hang* on. I've got it. Lydia!'

'*Lydiaaa*,' said Anne and Julian in harmony.

George let out a long, satisfied sigh. This was all highly amusing.

'But what do we call her, though? Seriously,' said Julian. 'Grandma? Nanna? Nan? Granny? Grams?'

'No way to tell,' said Dick. 'Let's cut our losses and call her Gran.'

Having made this momentous contribution, Dick spent the rest of the journey playing a game on his phone, where he was a juicy blackcurrant jumping along a branch over a never-ending sequence of sharp thorns and devouring maggots. So far, he had amassed a personal best-score of 2,465,822 and was enjoying himself about as much as a person can.

George and Anne, not being boys, had brought sensible things to do. Anne was knitting a toy for Lily, their beloved niece, while listening to *Woman's Hour* on her smartphone.

George was supposed to be catching up on work, but was continuously distracted by WhatsApp messages from friends. Flipping continuously from laptop to phone and back, she certainly *looked* busy, but as the train passed Doncaster, she realized that, so far in the journey, she had eaten four bags of crisps, and had written just a single email. Her gaze settled on the name of the town they were travelling through, and she reflected sadly that this was where her cousins' grandmother was buried. . .

'Wait a minute, you bastards,' she said, gaining the attention of the entire quiet carriage, 'she's not your bloody grandmother! What is this bullshit?'

'Keep it down, George!' whispered Julian urgently, leaning over the table and tucking his paperback under his arm. He looked mortified.

'But I just worked it out. She's *not* your gran!' replied

'Hang on,' said Dick. 'What's Gran's actual name?'

George, now speaking much quieter than before. 'Your grandmother passed away back in the sixties.'

'I got some more ciders,' said Dick, sitting back next to her. 'What have you guys been yelling about? Everyone's looking at us. I thought you said the silence of the Quiet Carriage was sacrosanct, Julian? Equivalent to the medieval peasant setting foot inside Chartres Cathedral?'

'Oh, *shut up*,' said Julian. 'George has hit upon a bullseye of family goss, and that supersedes all. Anne tells it better than me.'

Dick nodded, and keeping his thumb pressed over the seal, cracked open a cider as quietly as he could.

Anne, granted official licence to gossip, transformed from innocent angel into scurrilous muckspreader in the bat of an eyelid. '*Well*,' she said, taking a deep breath.

'Our actual grandmother died when mummy was very little, and grandad married again when he was in his sixties, just after Julian was born. So mummy never really saw Granny B as a mother, but of course when we were little, she was the only grandma we knew, on that side of the family.'

'That's *right*,' said Julian. 'I'd almost forgotten.'

'So she's not actually related to any of us?' said George. 'But wait. Wasn't there something funny about her will?'

Julian opened his mouth to answer, but Anne was back in like a bullet.

'*Yes*,' she said. 'There was always this mystery about Granny B – that she had two previous husbands who had left her their inheritances. And then grandad passed away twenty years ago, and she married again soon after. But she's just one of those people who hates to travel, and has always refused to spend money. She still lives in the tiny house she grew up in before the war.

'Rumour has it she's got an enormous fortune hidden away in there somewhere – and that she has no will, either. So any especially kind visitor who makes her life better might, perhaps, find themselves richer to the tune of . . .' She looked out of the train window. 'Who knows?' she asked, and went back to her knitting, while George and Julian stared out at the landscape.

'Three million!' cried Dick jubilantly, looking up from his phone.

Julian and George both jumped. Anne flinched and missed a stitch, then tutted and looked crossly over at Dick. 'Don't you think you've had enough of those endlessly replenishing ciders?'

Dick, who *had* had enough of those ciders, said, with a

slight furriness in his voice, that he rather thought he hadn't, and rose to go to the buffet car.

Anne turned to Julian to make some sort of averagely unhelpful remark, which he would pay no heed to anyway, and stopped, because he was grinning at her with childish excitement.

'We're here!' he said.

They all looked out of the windows as the train slowed. It was hard to make out much of the town through the driving rain, which was energetically thrashing itself against the window. But then there was no denying the large white sign on the platform, reading *ACCLINGTON*.

'That must be her,' said Julian.

On the platform stood a woman in a see-through plastic mac with matching galoshes, see-through umbrella and see-through plastic shower cap. She saw them, and they saw her, all at once. They all waved madly.

'Woof!' said Timmy, jumping up.

CHAPTER THREE

Granny B

The four housemates, caught unawares by the suddenness of the stop, bundled themselves off the train in a rush, and on to the platform. Then Granny B was saying hello, and they were smiling and saying hello back, laughing and giving kisses.

Gran seemed physically tiny. This was to be expected because, over the last twenty years, she'd shrunk a bit and they'd grown a lot. Nevertheless, now they were in front of her, it was astounding. She looked like she could fit inside Julian's rucksack, with plenty of room to spare.

There was something else that each of them felt most strikingly at setting eyes on her again – it had been so long that they hardly recognized her. This made them feel terribly guilty, and they overcompensated with exclamations of affection.

'Oh, that's nice, that's lovely,' Gran said, smiling beneath a welter of hugs. 'It's nice to see you all. You're so big!'

'Woof!' said Timmy.

'Except for you, Pongo; you're still the same size,' Gran said.

'Woof!' said Timmy, in protest at this new name. But the housemates' collective guilt had yet to be assuaged, and none could bring themselves to correct her.

'I wish I could drive you,' Gran said, 'but I've no car, I'm afraid. It's not much of a walk, though, if you don't mind the rain. Come on, Pongo!'

Acclington was a Lancashire town that hunched along the side of a hill, seemingly to try to escape the incessant rain that lashed it from the Irish Sea. Terraces of narrow brick cottages on cobbled streets rose, one above the other, up the hill's steep gradient, like scales on the side of an enormous dragon. Windows glowed orange in the late afternoon gloom, and the smoke drifted contentedly from a few dozen chimneys, making for the impression that here was a town that would have been rejected by the producers of the old Hovis adverts, for being a bit OTT.

The cottage, when they found themselves in front of it, didn't seem dramatically larger than Gran herself. Found two-thirds along one of the ubiquitous terraces, its door opened directly on to the cobbles. Within was a world of doilies, pungent and arguing smells, and disorder.

They all tried to make vague murmurs of pleasure as they entered, although in each case these quickly died away into silence or took on a dubious tone. Julian, coming last, simply whispered, '*What the hell?*' under his breath.

'Don't mind the mess,' Gran said. 'I do let things get on top of me when Stan's away . . .'

There was an armchair, bulging with unopened post, next to a gas fire and two heaters going full blast. It seemed a recipe for disaster, and ready to go up at any moment. Not that catching fire would cause a significant increase in the temperature. It was close to unbearably hot, and the four immediately got to work removing layers to try to reduce perspiration.

But at least they wouldn't dehydrate; from the moment they first crossed the threshold, to when they left several days later, they were never without a cup of tea. Making (she called it 'mashing') and serving tea was, for Gran, a mania – almost a religious obsession. She made tea in the way a superstitious Roman matriarch might cross herself, which is to say she did it in response to feelings of gratitude, remorse, jubilation, despair, boredom and ill temper. Like

George and Anne, not being boys, had brought sensible things to do.

any habit, she often did it without thinking, and sometimes in rising to make a cup, would nearly upset the full one she had just poured.

Before the four housemates had managed to get their jumpers off and find a seat, therefore, the kettle was rumbling and the pot was being warmed. There was a hatch from the miniature kitchen that looked into the undersized living room, and through this Gran carried on talking while they struggled to find a place to sit down.

'You're all looking so healthy!' she said. 'And Pongo – my, you look good for your age. In dog years, you must be older than me!'

'Woof!' agreed Timmy, always gratified to have his great age acknowledged.

'What are you all up to, these days?'

As they brought her up to date on their C.V.s, the visitors looked around and tried to identify the peculiar smell. The top note was sickly sweet, as though someone had won a bottle of perfume at the fair and then accidentally spilt it down the back of the sofa. The second element was of accumulated dust, some of which had burnt on the fire and the half-dozen heaters that were tucked around the room. Through all ran the faint but penetratingly rank odour that might result from a lamb chop having slipped and bounced beneath an armchair, unnoticed, in 1991.

The smell was sharpened by the stifling heat, and actually made George think she was going to pass out. To avoid this embarrassment, she took her bag and Anne's upstairs. She placed them in the alarmingly minuscule spare room, thinking to herself, Well, that will be cosy. I guess Anne and I will know each other a bit better by the end of the weekend.

By the time she came down, everyone had caught up with each other's lives and conversation was starting to pall. Both parties were beginning to realize they were essentially stuck with a stranger, and wondering what to say next.

'So, what will you do this weekend?' Gran asked, smiling. 'What would you like to get up to?'

The four had not even begun to think this far ahead. Visiting someone normally came with an inherent list of things to do – usually pre-arranged by the host. They smiled blankly.

Then Julian said: 'Well, it would be nice to take you out for lunch on Sunday. Perhaps a roast?'

'Oh, not for me,' Gran said. 'I don't like being made a fuss of.'

Anne looked sharply over at Julian, knowing his hatred

of sentences that end with a preposition, and his inability to curb his tongue. She saw his jaw working as he grappled with his own instinct, but he overcame it.

'And besides, I hardly seem to eat anything, these days,' Gran went on. 'You should all go out for a nice walk, though. There are lovely walks around these parts. The town was a favourite haunt of the Brontë sisters, you know. They used to come here to buy calico . . .'

As Julian understood it, there wasn't a town in this part of the world which *hadn't* been favoured by the Brontës in some 'wise' (as they might have put it) and subsequently exploited for the purposes of tourism. Any truth in the matter of the Brontës' affection had long ago stopped being even part of the point. He promised Gran they would be sure to go for a good long hike.

'So, where's your husband?' Dick asked. 'We've never met him!'

'Stan's off at another of his conferences,' Gran said. 'Every year, at this time, like clockwork, he has to spend a week delivering lectures – and listening to them, poor devil. When he's away, everything seems to go to pot round here – I rely on him for so much.'

'I say,' said Julian. 'Is there anything we can help with?'

22

*Gran seemed physically tiny. This was to be expected
because, over the last twenty years, she'd shrunk a bit
and they'd grown a lot.*

'Oh, no,' Lydia said. 'Don't be silly. It's lovely just to have you here.'

'But there must be *something*,' Dick insisted. 'It's the least we can do, after all.'

'Well . . .' Gran looked towards the back of the house, and they were pleased to see she was wavering. 'There is my computer . . .' she said. 'I could do with some help on that . . .'

'Then help on that is what we will give!' said Julian.

'Woof!' said Timmy.

So it began.

CHAPTER FOUR

Of Course We Can Help with the Computer

When they enquired, it turned out there were various things that Granny B needed help with on her computer. She wanted to set up an iTunes account so she could download and listen to 'some of the old records I used to have', as a friend had recently told her that all the old music was now available digitally.

When she talked about the old records, her face became suddenly animated, as though she could remember the first time she had heard them. When asked to name the artists, however, she became vague, and started humming and tapping her fingers as an aide memoire.

'The Everly Brothers,' she said. 'The Beverley Sisters …'

'Is that two separate groups, or were you correcting yourself?'

But Lydia was lost in a fog of fond remembrance. Once she had started, the names came out of her non-stop, and George struggled to keep up.

'Jim Reeve, Pat Boone ...'

'Wait!' said George. 'I'm three behind. What was that previous one, who sounded like Jim Morrison?'

Gran looked blank.

'Not Jim Morrison,' said George, 'I meant *Van* Morrison.'

'Who?' asked Gran.

George struggled. 'Maybe I was thinking of Val Doonican?' she asked.

'Oh!' Lydia said. 'You mean Lonnie Donegan. Yes, he was marvellous.'

'If you say so,' said George, making a note. 'But actually, I think we're straying from the point. We can make a list later. First things first, let's just set up the account. Now, what operating system does your P.C. run on?'

'Electricity,' said Gran. 'Honestly, this is very kind of you ...'

She led them to the back of the house, where what had once been a poky laundry room was now an absurdly small office. They squeezed into it, with Dick sitting on a small filing cabinet, Anne squatting on the floor and George leaning in the doorway.

The computer was an impressively large piece of machinery that smelt even more sharply of burnt dust than the rest of the house. It was of a make that Julian had never seen before. There were shoe boxes piled left and right, spilling over with old cassettes, post-it notes, staplers and the like. Everywhere else were great lengths of wires and plugs of every kind. Next to the chair on the floor was a large sloppy pile of telephone directories.

The first thing Julian did was to turn the computer on; the second was to remove a coffee cup from the disc tray, allowing it to close.

'Is that not what it's for?' asked Lydia.

'Not really,' said Julian. 'So, tell me, what's your email address?'

'Here they are,' said Gran. She pointed to a ragged sheet, pinned to the wall. It was torn from the back of a seed catalogue and covered with scribbles in a tiny hand and in many different colours of ink.

Julian squinted at it, turning it round and round, and then twisted the neck of a lamp so he could get a clearer look. With difficulty, he read an email address aloud.

'Yes,' she said. 'That's it.'

'You're sure? There are quite a few on here.'

'No, that's definitely it.'

Julian set to work. First, he decided to do a test run. He

*Within was a world of doilies, pungent smells,
and disorder.*

went round the house finding a handful of CDs that Lydia might like to have digitized and available on her iPod.

When he had the music piled up in front of him, he looked through the collection and let out a sigh. It mainly comprised of northern colliery marching bands, soundtracks to West End musicals, and classical music compilations with track listings like *Carmina Burana – Carl Orff (Heineken advert)*. Nevertheless, the music was soon uploaded on to iTunes and present in the library.

'Okay!' said Julian. 'Next step.' He took the proffered iPod and plugged it in.

'So, what are you doing now?' Lydia asked. 'I want to try and be able to do all this myself.'

'Of course,' said Julian. 'So, we've plugged in your iPod, here. And you see it comes up here, in the sidebar, as a device. It's labelled *WifePod*.'

'Why is it called that?'

'Call me Sherlock Holmes, but I suspect it's because your husband gave it that name.'

'Oh, of course,' Lydia said, with a chuckle. She leant forward, peering through her specs with a birdlike expression.

'You see it?' Julian asked, pointing with the cursor.

Although Gran nodded, through the corner of his eye,

Julian noticed her gaze wandering aimlessly over the screen. He jabbed at it with his finger.

'Oh, yes, there!' Gran said.

'Good. Now we're going to sync the device – "sync" as in "synchronize". That just means put things on to this iPod from the computer.'

'Slow down,' Gran said.

'Okay,' said Julian. 'By clicking on *WifePod*, here, it shows us, over *here*, everything that's on your device. You see? There's nothing on it at all, except a few audiobooks, and some photos.'

'Don't look at those,' said Gran.

'We can't,' Julian explained. 'All we can see from here is an overview of what's using up the memory on your device. Like a, a portfolio, if you like. This is where we manage what goes on to your iPod.'

Julian smiled at her. She nodded seriously, looking at the screen.

'You see, everything that's on your iPod comes from the computer. It's stored here, and we put it on *there*.'

Julian was starting to loathe the sound of his own voice. 'To get these songs on your iPod,' he said, bucking himself up with a burst of fake cheerfulness, 'we go to *Music* and tick the albums we want. Like ... er ... this one. *Cliff Richard Sings Another 101 Christmas Carols*. Then we click *Sync*. And then – look – all those tracks are transferring across to your device now.'

'That's it?' Lydia asked.

'That's it!' Julian said, jubilantly. He never wanted to talk to anyone about computers ever again. Even this brief conversation had turned him half demented.

Gran sighed with relief that it was over. 'Thank goodness,' she said. 'You are so nice to me. Anyone for tea?' Then she leant over and switched the P.C. off at the plug.

The four housemates watched the screen blink out as the hard-drive made a noise like a strangulated chaffinch. They heard the click of the kettle being put on in the next room.

'Woof?' asked Timmy.

CHAPTER FIVE

Vista of Frustration

Everyone moved back to the front room to reacquaint themselves with its sweltering heat and enjoy their fourth cup of tea of the afternoon. The one member of the group who really enjoyed this was Timmy, who (having found a pile of newspapers to curl up on) had decided the house's many intriguing smells could wait until tomorrow for investigation. He was, for now, content to slide into a gentle afternoon nap, which he was more than happy to turn into an evening snooze, followed by a full-on night-time sleepathon. Timmy had never gone in for laziness on this scale before, but as he had a good stretch and a yawn, and felt the blanket of warmth snuggle comfortably around him, he wondered if he had not in fact earned it, after all these years . . .

Having handed out the cups of tea, Granny B sat back and looked at her guests. They were all engrossed in their phones. George was leaving (no doubt perfectly balanced and reasonable) comments on the *Guardian* website; Anne was surreptitiously reading a wedding dresses subreddit, and creating a top-ten wish list; Dick was improving still further on his high score in the blackcurrant escape game (which was called *Maggot Run*™); and Julian was trying and failing to find out the scores from the second day of the Test in Sri Lanka, and waving his phone in the air.

With no conversation on offer from her visitors, Gran took up her own device and began to explore its contents.

'Oh, no,' she said. 'No, no, no; this can't be right. Please, tell me it's not.'

She seemed like she might be about to cry, and they all looked at her in disbelief.

'What is it?' Julian asked.

'My audiobooks,' she said. 'They're not on here!'

Julian felt his gut churn.

'But they're my most treasured thing!' she said.

The grandchildren all gathered round, assuring her it would be okay. Julian was horrified that he had been instrumental in removing works of literature from anyone, and examining the device only deepened his guilt. They simply were not there.

They all decamped to the computer room, teacups trembling in hands. As calmly and plainly as possible, given her agitated state, it was explained to Granny B that the main problem with her iPod came from her turning the machine off at the mains. A computer should always be turned off correctly, they told her, allowing it to finish doing its work, and so that it knew that everything inside was 'put away correctly'. As they told her this she looked at them with an expression of suspended disbelief, like a too-old child being told about the working practices of the Tooth Fairy.

At the end she nodded tensely, and everyone avoided each other's eyes as the P.C. finished booting up.

Julian was about to take the seat in front of the computer, but hesitated.

'Let me take over,' said George, to Julian's relief. She jumped into the chair, patted Lydia reassuringly on the knee and asked Julian to fill everyone's teacups again.

She clicked through various menus and settings for a good few minutes, looking increasingly concerned, and then said, 'Well, of course this thing isn't bloody working properly. All these systems are completely incompatible.'

'Explain?' asked Anne, sipping her tea.

'This P.C. is running on Windows 5,' said George, 'which is impossibly ancient. The iPod has a version of iOS that even the Neanderthals would have found frustrating. And the

Making and serving tea was, for Gran, a mania.

hardware they are trying to communicate through, although modern by comparison with Stephenson's Rocket or the spinning jenny, is in fact incredibly shit and old. Pardon my French, Gran.'

'Oh, I've heard much worse,' said Lydia. 'Now, I think I'll just leave you to it . . .'

'Wait, wait,' said George. 'Can I please update the operating system on this machine? Then everything will run much more smoothly.'

Granny B nodded. 'Of course, if it will help,' she said.

George proceeded to download Windows 10. She did not know yet know that 'run much more smoothly' was a phrase that would ring painfully in her ears.

CHAPTER SIX

Signal Failure

Dick and Anne might have advised George against this course of action, had they really been listening. However, they were not, and so, like many hapless innocents before her, George commenced the download of Windows 10, trusting that it would put everything right.

Julian, meanwhile, was becoming increasingly agitated by his failure to get a signal (the house did not have Wi-Fi), which was preventing him from checking the cricket score. Despite the fact that he could have looked on the computer, or switched on the radio or television, or simply asked someone, Julian had decided that it was the principle of the thing, and was now whipping himself up into an enjoyably self-righteous temper.

How could it be, he asked himself, as he went out the front door and crossed the road, that in this day and age, in a reasonably large conurbation such as Acclington, there was no working mobile signal? He held his phone up as high as he could and jumped up and down. He saw a hand go to a net curtain in a nearby window, and one of the neighbours peaked out.

'Hello!' he said, waving merrily. The hand withdrew and the curtain fell back into place. So much for warm-hearted and welcoming northerners. He looked at his phone again: nothing.

He walked to the end of the street and proceeded down the hill to the main road. He stood by the roundabout and jumped up and down a few times until a car stopped, a window lowered and a nice couple asked if he wanted a lift.

'Oh, no,' Julian laughed. 'I'm sorry. I was just, er . . . Look, you don't know the best place to get a phone signal round here, do you?'

'Beg pardon?'

'Oh, er, nothing. Thank you, though!' He waved as they pulled away, both of them clearly confused, and realized he should just have asked them what the bloody cricket score was. How did he get himself into these situations?

He was now far too deep into this to admit defeat. Common sense told him that, somewhere between here and Hadrian's Wall, his phone would pick up a signal. And he intended to prove this, even if it meant death from exposure and starvation. To avoid attracting any further attention, Julian headed away, off the main road, down a quieter, more rural-looking lane, with a broad grass verge bounded by a sturdy wooden fence.

Wanting to gain greater height, Julian made for the fence and heaved himself up on to it. Here, he balanced precariously and uncomfortably, the narrow wooden slats pinching the skin of his thighs. He held the phone up. Then, having a new idea, he threw it thirty feet into the air and, clutching hard on to the fence with his spare hand, caught it as it came down. He wasn't a fan of cricket for nothing, after all. He looked at the screen.

One bar.

'YES!' he shouted, thrusting both arms into the air, losing his balance, and falling off the fence into the field on the other side.

The ground rushed up and thumped the wind out of him, but after staggering to his feet and patting himself down, he found he was in one piece and not much harmed. What's more, he had missed a very large and predominantly liquid cowpat by just a few inches. Then he saw what was in the middle of the cowpat.

'Let's get you cleaned up,' he said, carefully picking

'In dog years, you must be older than me,' said Gran.

the phone out of the surprisingly sweet-smelling sludge and wiping it on the wet grass. He wondered how exactly he would word any insurance claim that might ensue, and looked around for anywhere he might carefully clean the phone. Then, across the field and through a hole in the hedge, he saw a car park, and attached to the car park he saw the brooding thatched roof of an old-fashioned pub, its lights starting to glow warmly in the afternoon's encroaching murk.

'Victory!' Julian said, holding his phone aloft.

CHAPTER SEVEN

Further Computer Woes

George had watched Julian's marshalling of the grandparental computer with an enjoyable build-up of scorn. The guy just didn't know what he was doing. So she had been relieved when she got the chance to take over, and had sat down with complete confidence.

This confidence was now but a memory.

'So where are my audiobooks?' Gran was asking.

'They're on the computer . . .' George said cautiously.

'Right,' said Gran. 'So you've found them.'

'Not exactly,' said George. 'But they must be somewhere . . .'

'Stan had just downloaded the new Martina Cole for me,' said Lydia plaintively. 'I do so like her.'

'We'll get them back; we'll get them all back. I promise. I just . . . It'll take me a while to get used to this new set-up. Is it your husband who usually looks after all this?'

'Yes,' Gran nodded.

'You seem terribly distressed,' said George.

'I am,' said Lydia.

'Would you look this way?' George asked, holding up her phone. 'That's lovely. Thank you. That'll convince them back at work. Now, let's try to log into iTunes to get these audiobooks back . . .'

'They'll be on Audible,' Dick said without looking up from his phone. 'Look in the Audible folder.'

'But I've *looked* in the Audible folder, Dick,' said George through gritted teeth.

'I'll make us all a nice cup of tea,' said Gran, leaving.

'Look,' said Dick, 'if you can't find where they are, just log in afresh and leave them downloading overnight. Then tomorrow morning – bingo. There they will be. And we can bung them on her iPod.'

'Sounds sensible,' said Anne.

'Fine,' said George. 'We just need to find which email address is the right one, then.'

Anne picked up the seed-catalogue scrap again, and the three of them painstakingly went over the whole page, reading out every email address they could see. What made the experience somewhat bewildering was the number of pseudonyms that Granny B had used in the last twenty years.

They knew, for instance, that Grandad Barnard – their blood relation – had passed away long ago, after which Lydia (Granny B, his second wife) had made a deeply affecting deathbed marriage to a dear old friend from her youth, who had passed away soon after. Then, as far as they could tell, Granny B had met and married her present husband.

However, the Kirrin children had been so inattentive to their grandmother this past decade that they could not remember exactly which name was which. They were too embarrassed to admit to anyone but each other the depth of their ignorance.

To look at them, the names on the sheet could be genuine names, nicknames, intentional noms de plume or code names using monickers of favourite pets.

Rather than speculate fruitlessly, then, they ploughed ahead trying all the addresses and passwords available, with Dick and Anne deciphering the crabby scrawl and George typing the names into Audible, incorporating multiple spellings based on the highly variable interpretation of the dubious handwriting on offer.

'Got one!' said George. 'Look! Here it is. Great. Oh. Look what's on here.'

'What operating system does your P.C. run on?'
'Electricity,' said Gran.

'Don't tell me it's erotica,' said Anne. 'Just don't *tell* me. I can't bear to hear it.' She stuffed her fingers in her ears and started humming.

'No, don't be stupid, Anne. The only two books downloaded on this account are *Scotland's Second-Hardest Bastard*, and *Diana: The Truth At Last??* – with two question marks.'

'Doesn't sound like her,' said Dick. 'More like hubby.'

'Keep looking, then. Next email address?'

'La, la, la – not listening to you,' said Anne.

'It's OKAY ANNE; THERE'S NO PORN!' yelled Dick. Then he added, 'Christ, I hope Gran didn't hear that.'

It would be going too far to say that Julian had been an instantaneous hit in the Stoat and Cudgel, the medieval stone-walled public house he had stumbled into with his poo-smeared phone.

Like any upper-middle-class Englishman, his slightly plummy accent rarely gained him the instant sympathy of a group of pub regulars. But there were factors in his favour. One was that, although he at first struck them as an outsider, they quickly saw he was a pubman through and through. This was a kinship that crossed class divides, and when they perceived this, they warmed to him quicker than if he had been a rough-souled, flat-capped northerner in the first place.

Second was that, making no secret of entering the pub as he did, brandishing a cowshit-besmeared iPhone, which he went to the toilets to clear up, he generated a lot of amusement at the bar on an otherwise quiet afternoon.

Third was that he was so delighted to find this beacon of civility in the mist-shrouded hills, he instantly bought everyone a drink ('everyone' being, at that moment, Greg the Landlord, Geoff, Old Geoff, Ted, Greek Sonya and Angry Terry the Dog.)

Thus, when he rolled home at about dinner time, he was in a noticeably improved mood. Because the others were still trying to sort out the computer, he went and sat in the kitchen with Gran, while she prepared dinner. He did his best to ignore her repeated comments about how this was 'unusually late for her' (it was half past six) and plugged his laptop into his portable modem.

Meanwhile, Kirrin Group #2, at the computer, at last felt that they were not so far from being on the right track. They were pretty sure they had located the correct account for Gran's

Everyone moved back to the front room to reacquaint themselves with its sweltering heat and enjoy their fourth cup of tea of the afternoon.

audiobooks, and presently they started to re-download all the titles that she was missing from her iPod. There was a collective breath of relief.

Now she had downloaded Windows 10, the last thing that remained was for George to allow the new operating system to be implemented on the machine. This she did with a glad click, allowing the P.C. to restart, before switching it off.

God, George thought. Why is it that people in this country make such a big deal about getting used to computers, and new technology? It's not like it's such a big shift . . .

Anne and Dick came through to the kitchen, to find Gran leaning over Julian's laptop, chuckling away at all the videos she had found of cats on the internet. 'Oh, *look* at this one!' she said.

'Where's Julian?' Anne asked.

'Just in the other room. Going through my post for me. Don't go, dinner's nearly ready!'

George, Anne and Dick knew very well what tended to happen if Julian went off in the middle of the afternoon on an apparently innocuous task and didn't return for ages. So, ignoring Gran's imprecations, they proceeded to the front room with suspicions raised. They saw Julian returning from the front door, yawning and stretching his arms.

'Job done!' he said.

'What job, Julian?' asked Anne.

'Gran asked me to go through her post. Turns out she gets absolutely tonnes of junk mail, addressed to all sorts of weirdos.'

'I *do* find it hard to get to grips with things . . .' said Lydia. 'When Stan's not here. I'm very grateful, Julian. It *is* reassuring having you here.'

The others looked at Julian, who beamed somewhat bluntly back at them all. They were far from convinced that whatever he was up to was the least bit helpful.

'Dinner's served!' said Gran.

'Woof,' said Timmy sleepily, roused from his all-day snooze.

CHAPTER EIGHT

Good Old-fashioned Cooking

At dinner, Julian was somewhat clumsy in his movements and reticent of speech, but as they all crammed round the table in the kitchen, the others felt a soaring of spirits. After all, everyone knew there was nothing like the cuisine of one's maternal ancestry. If one's mother's cooking was profoundly reassuring, surely a grandmother's cooking must be the same thing, but cubed? One stage closer to heaven? Something almost transcendent, that might be called manna?

'One for you,' said Gran, dunking a Fray Bentos pie on George's plate. 'And one for you, one for you ...'

They looked at these hardened, dark-brown parcels, like clay pucks, and reserved judgement. None of them had eaten one before, after all. And perhaps they were supposed to be burnt?

'Gravy,' said Gran unnecessarily, brandishing a gravy boat of pale brown liquid that looked like run-off from the washing machine, except for the gluey dots in it, which gave the impression of drowned ants. The universal feeling amongst the ingrates, as the gravy was ladled over their black-brown pastry dinner, was that a couple more stirs in the jug wouldn't have gone amiss.

These delicacies were followed by watery mash and a baby's handful of frozen veg, overcooked to a buttery softness. Even Dick, who was prepared to undergo severe privation rather than make a fuss, glanced around the kitchen desperately for condiments.

'It might not be quite what you are used to getting down south,' Gran said.

'No, no,' said Dick vaguely, messing around with the food on his plate until Gran was looking in another direction, and glancing under the table for Timmy.

'Yum,' said George flatly, piercing the surface of the pastry with the resounding crack of a boundary cover-drive.

Anne was affronted by her housemates' failure to appreciate their generous dinner. She got three or four mouthfuls down her before discreetly pinching her nose and closing her eyes as she repressed a heave.

'Is that the door?' asked Julian.

'Oh, is it?' asked Gran.

There was a scramble of activity in the kitchen as she tottered to the door, looked outside and came back.

'No one there. Oh! You must have been famished,' she said, looking at the four empty plates in front of her, rather than the four guilty faces above them. She also failed (or refused) to hear the sound of ravenous canine activity from beneath the table.

'That was *lovely*,' Anne said, smilingly sweetly; but, keen to push the conversation along, she added, 'I say, I *am* full, Granny, darling, and oh-so sleepy. Where's the second bedroom for the boys?'

'Second bedroom,' Gran repeated, settling to her own meal.

They all watched her, expecting her to follow this up with another remark, like, 'Second bedroom? It's in the attic,' or, 'It's the old converted bomb shelter, at the back of the garden.' As the silence extended, they found they would have settled for, 'It's a tad cosy, but the old coal shed has just about room for two.'

But instead Gran patiently shovelled mouthful after mouthful of mash and pie down her, looking up at them occasionally, until it was all gone. By now, it began to dawn on the four of them that this wasn't a delaying tactic so much as a conversational one. Her silence was intended to speak for itself – there was no answer.

Anne realized that the bedroom George had thought was very small for two people was going to have to do for four.

'The bedroom might be a bit cramped,' Gran admitted, 'but it's just the way houses were built up here, in the old days. You always used to fit up there. That room slept seven in the Blitz, after all!'

Half a dozen sarcastic replies danced on the tip of Julian's tongue, where they were entertained briefly, before being swallowed, along with his pride. In turn, and despite the wretchedly early hour, all four housemates came to terms with their identical fate and headed to the stairs.

After all taking turns in the small, cold bathroom, the two women settled down to sleep on the bed, with Dick and Julian on the floor. It was absurdly early, but if Lydia was going to sleep then they might as well too.

'Lights out,' Anne said primly at the stroke of nine.

Darkness fell across them, almost immediately accompanied by the snoring of George.

'Blitz spirit, my backside,' said Julian, wriggling to try and remove the crick from his neck. 'German bombers never came this far north.'

Julian was becoming increasingly agitated by his failure to get a signal, which was preventing him from checking the cricket score.

'They did, actually,' came Gran's muffled voice, through the wall.

'*Shush*, Julian,' Anne whispered.

'Woof,' agreed Timmy.

In the dark, Julian blushed invisibly.

CHAPTER NINE

Proper Tea is Theft

The next morning, they came downstairs to find Granny B ready with a freshly brewed pot of tea. After a nine-hour break, this first cup of the day was at least quite welcome. Lydia then suggested a nice walk on the fells.

Julian looked out the front window, across the valley, as the last shreds of mist were being burnt off the hills by the autumn sunshine. He had a dull ache between his temples that would surely be helped by a brisk walk in the fresh air.

'Or we could go to the Old Watermill, just a mile away,' said Anne. 'It sells a rather nice range of knitwear, I see online . . .'

'There's a rock-climbing academy across town I wouldn't mind going to have a look at,' said George. 'Some of the most difficult walls in the country.'

'We're not going gallivanting around the countryside until we've fixed Gran's computer,' said Dick. 'First things first.'

'What a nice grandson you are,' said Anne.

'Not really,' Dick observed. 'So far, all we've done is make things worse. I'm not having Gran being down on our visit, for God's sake – the least we can do is bring her back to a net par.'

The others could not disagree with this logic.

So they got to work.

Granny B hovered behind their shoulders and asked if she could help, but once George had started poking around on the machine, and discovered, to her consternation, that she had no idea where anything was, they decided it would be best if Gran left them alone, for the time being.

'I'll just busy myself in the kitchen,' she said. 'Put the kettle on.'

For the first half hour, George pulled her hair out. Microsoft 10 seemed designed to befuddle and infuriate, even while it pretended to be your new best friend (which made things much worse). Eventually, Anne told George to go outside and take deep breaths, which she did, and Anne sat down to replace her. She called Lydia through from the next room.

'Why don't I set you up with online utilities accounts, darling Gran?' Anne asked. 'Get your electricity, phone, gas and so on – all in the same name? Then you can pay your bills at the click of a button!'

'Oh, is that really necessary?' Gran asked. 'I'm not sure I'd know how.'

'That doesn't matter,' said Anne brightly. '*I* know how. I can leave my mobile number here and you can phone me if you have any questions. Honestly, it's dead easy. Once you get used to it, you won't look back.'

Lydia gave a slow nod that was grateful and wary in equal measure.

'Okay,' said Anne, turning back to the computer. 'Here we go . . .' She began tapping. And, in anticipation of the offer, she asked if she might possibly have a cup of rooibos tea.

'Rubbish tea?' asked Gran.

'No, it's – oh, please don't worry,' Anne said, suddenly self-conscious.

'Is that a special type of tea?' Gran asked. 'I've got lots. They don't just sell Tetley up here, you know.'

'Oh!' said Anne, brightening. 'How about white tea?'

'Of course,' said Gran. 'We've got milk.'

'No, no,' said Anne, embarrassed again. 'Er – do you have camomile?'

Gran looked down at her hands.

'Lemon?' Anne asked. 'Ginger? Red berry? Jasmine?'

Timmy was more than happy for his afternoon nap to turn into an evening snooze, followed by a full-on night-time sleepathon.

Lydia's defensive expression not altering, Anne started to flail desperately. 'Liquorice?'

'I've got some lemon barley . . .' Gran said.

'That would be SMASHING!' Anne nearly yelled, desperate for the conversation to be over.

As Gran sidled away, Anne turned to the computer again, with a determined expression.

CHAPTER TEN

We Have Sent You a Password-resetting Email

'I realize that, Rita,' said Anne patiently. 'No, I *do* realize that it's irregular. Is the name on the account now . . . ? Oh, thank you. And, as promised, I'll send through a scan of my grandmother's marriage certificate and mark the email for your notice. Thank you, Rita. You've been most helpful. How is the weather up there in Newcastle, by the way? Oh, it is? I'm so sorry. You have such a lovely voice, by the way. Oh, thank you. Goodbye.'

Anne terminated the telephone conversation and let out a long, tremolo sigh. She turned to look out of the tiny office window at the last remaining vestiges of what appeared to have been a rather nice afternoon. Hearing the kettle boiling next door, she went through and flopped on a kitchen chair.

'So,' she said. 'I've successfully changed your accounts for gas, water, electricity, phone and internet to your proper and current name. All sorted. Now I need to put in your correct bank-account details – which I couldn't find on the sheet.'

'Don't believe in them,' said Gran, pleasantly but firmly.

'Quite right; probably a security risk to write them d—' There was something in Gran's voice that made Anne stop.

At that moment, Dick and George wandered back in from walking Timmy, who ran to the front room to regain his throne of peaceful slumber.

'How were things here?' George asked.

'Well, Julian's been an enormous help, I must say,' sighed Anne.

'*De rien, mon brave*!' Julian carolled from the front room, where he was basking in the Caribbean heat and reading an Agatha Christie paperback. 'This tea won't drink itself, after all . . .'

'Actually, it's probably a blessing he's sat it out,' Anne admitted, 'because I have managed to get all Gran's accounts lined up, all in her proper name. It was quite a mess, and I've spent much of the afternoon on the phone to call centres in all the corners of the globe. But it's – oh, *thanks*, Gran, that's lovely, yes, drop of milk, no, no sugar, thank you – but it's all pretty much done and dusted now. All I need is her bank account details.'

'Good work, Anne,' said Dick approvingly.

'Don't believe in them,' said Gran, again.

'What do you mean, Lydia darling?' Anne asked, trusting that she was mistaken. 'That you "don't believe in them"? What don't you believe in?'

'There's an empty teacup in here!' called Julian.

'I'll make him a fresh one,' Gran said, heaving herself to her feet.

'And Mr Biscuit is late for his appointment with Mr Tummy!'

'That git pushes his luck,' said George. Dick nodded.

They watched Gran rinse the leaves out of the pot, then slosh in some hot water as the kettle came towards the boil, and go through the whole comforting rigmarole of preparing tea. They got a clear sense that she was avoiding Anne's question, and that she was disappointed, when she finally popped the cosy over the full pot, to turn and find them still watching her.

'Sorry,' she said. 'You asked me something. What don't I believe in? Oh, yes. Bank accounts.'

Dick laughed.

'Everyone has a bank account,' said George.

Anne covered her eyes.

If a mother's cooking was profoundly reassuring, surely a grandmother's cooking must be one stage closer to heaven? 'One for you,' said Gran, dunking a Fray Bentos pie on George's plate.

'Mr Biscuit!' called Julian again from the next room.

George went to explain to Julian about Ms Fist connecting with Mr Nosebone, but as she came into the living room, she found him staring up at her in bewilderment.

'That's weird,' he said.

'What?'

'Everything just turned off.'

CHAPTER ELEVEN

Post Post-modernist

Rather than try to come to grips with the bank-account revelation, the others allowed curiosity to draw them to the front room.

'Look,' said Julian, pressing the remote control. 'Telly cut off just as the half-time scores were about to come on. Heater, too – all of them!'

They looked around and saw that this was the case.

'Julian,' said George. 'When you threw out all those letters yesterday, who were they addressed to?'

'All sorts of weirdos,' he said. 'Former residents, I expect. Whole bunch of them – Stubbins, Ridley, Webster . . .'

'Oh, dear,' said Gran.

'Julian,' wailed Anne, 'there *aren't* any former residents. Gran's lived here for sixty years!'

'They're *all* you, Gran?' asked Julian, horrified. 'But it's not possible! When were you called Webster?'

'For a year in the fifties,' Lydia said. 'My first husband. Before I met your grandfather.'

'Here, look, I made a list,' said Julian. 'Consuela de Magalhães? That can't be you . . .'

Gran nodded sadly.

'A misguided holiday romance. It did happen in those days, you know. He told me he was a Portuguese baron, down on his luck. I should have guessed really – when I met him he was offering donkey rides on Blackpool beach. Had to get an annulment from the Pope, on that one.'

'Let me see,' said Julian, glancing back at his list. 'There was a Cressida de Montfort.'

'The late Baron de Montfort,' said Lydia. 'So handsome. But he hid his terrible gambling debts from me, and then suddenly went missing after a walk on the heath. There were reported sightings all over the world, but he was eventually declared dead in '74.'

'Cressida, though?'

'Cressida's my middle name,' said Gran, 'after an aunt on my father's side. Apparently it's very common in Carlisle. Or – you know – frequent.'

Anne, who rather resented her own unmarried status, eyed Gran up with something approaching awe.

'Grizelda Pickering,' said Julian, 'that *must* be a joke.'

'Jim Pickering was the man I married after your grand-father,' said Gran. 'He might not have had any title, but was a *true* gentleman. So sad – he was already ill, even at our wedding. Grizelda was his pet name for me. It was a joke, you're right – from Hattie Jacques' character in *Hancock's Half Hour*.'

None of them had the mildest idea what she was talking about. They were fixated instead on the implications of Julian's confession. 'And Eunice Stubbins,' said Julian. 'She was on *Coronation Street*, wasn't she?'

'That's Ena Sharples,' said George.

'That's my name *now*,' said Granny B.

'"*Eunice*"?' asked Julian.

'Eunice-Lydia,' said Gran.

'Hang on, hang on,' said Julian, running his hands through his hair. 'That last name – that was the one with the red banners around the letters.'

'That's really what I wanted your help with,' Gran said, 'more than the computer. Those letters with the warning symbol on them were starting to pile up, and I was afraid of them.'

'So,' said Anne, 'if I'm right, then I've managed to get

'I just don't believe in bank accounts,' said Gran.

all your accounts online, but you've no bank account to pay them with?'

'I'm sorry,' Lydia said, 'this is all my fault . . .'

'But we haven't been cut off, surely? I mean, surely not?' For some reason, it was Julian's pathetic repetition that brought home to everyone that this was exactly what had happened. They looked at the blank screen of the telly, sensed the afternoon gloom starting to invade from outside. Even the blasting heat was starting to lose some of its furnace-like intensity.

'Of course not,' said Gran. 'I've just put the kettle on. Listen!'

They all paid attention to the stony silence that reigned through the house, interrupted only by the gentle snoring (or farting, given they were aurally identical) of Timmy the dog.

'I just don't believe in bank accounts,' said Gran, looking both defiant and defensive – and entirely vulnerable.

Anne, George, Dick and Julian saw her expression, and couldn't bear it. Without a word or a look passing between them, they knew that (having failed at all others since they arrived) they had but one task to perform. If it cost them their lives, they would get Gran a bank account, link all of her utilities to it, and make bloody well sure she understood how to use it, before the weekend was done.

Which, it being Saturday afternoon, presented a ticklish logistical challenge.

'Okay, the electricity's off,' said Anne. 'We can sort that. It's not the end of the world – you've still got gas.'

'They're all with the same company, these days,' said Lydia.

'It's quarter to four p.m.,' said George. 'And tomorrow is Sunday. Can we please get our arses in gear? Excuse my language, Gran.'

'Oh, don't you worry.'

'Gran,' said Anne. 'This may seem a personal question, but where's your post office account? And is your deposit book to hand? We'll have to move like lightning.'

'I told you,' said Gran. 'I don't believe in them.'

'You haven't even got a *post office* account?' Anne asked.

'*So where is your money*?' asked Julian, massaging the sides of his head.

'Come with me,' said Gran.

72

CHAPTER TWELVE

The Bank Job

In the cellar, to which Gran presently led them, all that was immediately visible was a higgledy-piggledy pile of leftover building materials, covered with dust and fluff to the thickness of a bear's hide, a bathtub filled with brown liquid and surrounded by plastic bottles and pipes, which was either a home brewery or a decidedly make-do-and-mend embalming kit, and some boxes of papers. There were about six boxes piled on top of each other, and it was to these that Gran pointed.

George and Anne gasped as they began looking through the top box.

'Sweet Christ,' said George.

'They're *all* full of money?' Anne asked, incredulously.

'Seems a lot, at first,' said Gran, 'but then, when you come to think of it, it's not much, really, for a whole life's savings.'

'How have you been paying your bills up till now?' Julian asked.

Gran opened her mouth to answer, but Julian cut her off. 'Actually, never mind that now,' he said. 'Come on – it's nearly four. Gran, I need some form of I.D. from you, please. Passport, birth certificate, that sort of thing.'

'I'll fetch it,' said Gran.

'Meantime,' said George, 'how the hell are we supposed to get all this cash to the bank? If someone stops us, it will be the mugging of the century.'

Anne looked at her watch. 'Less talking, more hauling,' she said. 'Julian, you help me with these. You two, go and find something to transport it in . . .'

'Left a bit!' shouted Julian. 'No! Left, you maniac! You're all over the road!'

Charged with finding a suitable vehicle for six cardboard boxes stuffed with hard cash, George and Dick ran into the street, looking for anything to help them.

At the end of the road was a piece of wasteland, from which they returned with a rusted supermarket trolley, with one wheel missing and two of its remaining ones bent. After running it up to the door, the boxes were laid in the trolley as inconspicuously as possible. There was precious little time for set-dressing, however, and so, as the four of them proceeded down the steep slope towards the high street, they all felt outrageously conspicuous, a situation not helped by Julian repeatedly shushing them at the top of his voice, casting scared looks over his shoulder and generally acting in the most suspicious way imaginable.

It seemed, however, that the street robbers of Lancashire had taken the afternoon off, because, despite the incredible gracelessness with which they manoeuvred the wonky shopping trolley down the hill, occasionally striking sparks off the cobbles with a metallic shriek, they were blessedly ignored by the locals.

'Now,' said Julian, as they took the corner on to the high street, which was still thronging with people in the late afternoon, 'do try to act as though these boxes are just full of old rubbish – nothing valuable at all. We don't want to attract attention.'

'Bollocks to that,' said George. 'We need to clear a path, and I know exactly how. FREE MONEY!' she bellowed.

Gran, who was trying to keep up with them, jumped as though she'd received an electric shock.

'Get your free money here!' cried George, reaching into

a box and waving a bunch of fivers over her head. 'No catch, no cheat, no problem; just come up to us and we'll give you a fiver!'

At this, everyone within a hundred yards discovered they had urgent business to attend to in the opposite direction, or on the other side of the street, and simply melted away.

'George!' said Julian, as the trolley proceeded down the high street entirely unmolested. 'You're a genius!'

They reached the doors of the local bank, just as a tubby man with the keys in his hands looked out on to the street, and made every appearance of being about to shut up shop.

'Don't even think about it, mate,' said Julian, dumping a cardboard box in his arms. 'You've just got your biggest new customer in a decade.'

It turned out, exactly as Julian had hoped, that if you make a significant enough deposit in the bank, they treat you rather specially.

Once the group had set foot inside, making it impossible (or at least extremely inconvenient) to get rid of them, and once the amount of money being handed over became apparent, the usual rules prevailing over the bank's opening hours were suspended.

There was an air of excitement in the bank, with much nervous laughter on both sides of the counter.

The manager, a balding, humorous woman in her fifties, made a space for these new customers to sit down, now that the regular ones had gone. She indicated to her tellers that overtime would be paid for the task of counting this vast sum of money. There was an air of excitement in the bank, with much nervous laughter on both sides of the counter.

When the counting had been going for half an hour and was less than a quarter completed, the manager came round to offer her guests a cup of tea or coffee. Julian wondered aloud whether there might be an 'office bottle of something or other' tucked away in a lower desk drawer somewhere, but was told with courteous severity that there wasn't. He settled, with bad grace, for a cup of Horlicks, then put his feet up on a nearby chair, plucked the Agatha Christie from his jacket pocket and sat reading and picking his nose while the counting continued a few feet away ...

CHAPTER THIRTEEN

Blackout

They returned to the house that night with great relief. Not a pleasant, rest-back-in-your-chair-and-bask-in-the-glow relief, however, more an inch-carefully-into-the-dark-house-and-hunt-in-cupboards-for-candles relief, which (the group soon discovered) was a good deal less relaxing than the first kind.

They had at least managed to get a bank account sorted for their grandmother. They were clinging to this as their chief and only accomplishment of the weekend. On the way home, Anne had stopped at a phone box (such things thankfully still existed in Acclington) and politely pestered the gas, electric and telephone providers into resuming service. At last, she received assurance that money had been received, so normal service would resume within the next twenty-four hours. There was nothing more that could be done.

When candles had been found, lit and distributed around

the place, and they had stopped barking their shins on the furniture, Lydia found some blankets and they settled into the front room, where the somnolent Timmy had not stirred from his slumbers for many hours, even despite the temperature's drop from tropical to merely extremely warm. The occupants of the house had no option, now, but to hunker down for a quiet evening together.

'Bit like the war, this,' said Gran. 'Of course, I was only little then, but it's funny how clearly you remember it. We often had to spend the night in a shelter, when the sirens sounded.'

'Must have been ghastly,' said Dick.

'Well, it was – but it was exciting too, if I'm honest. It made you feel part of something. That's what this generation lacks, I sometimes think . . .'

Oh, here we go, thought George.

Yes, she's *right*, thought Julian.

It must have been so exciting, having all those soldiers and flying aces dashing around, being all heroic, thought Anne.

I wonder if anyone's going to notice that fart, thought Dick. I can't blame Timmy *again*. What are they talking about anyway?

'But then came the sixties,' said Anne. 'I mean, weren't you roughly the right age to be ...'

Gran sniffed. 'That was all very well for fashionable London types who lived near Carnaby Street, but try getting away with any of that fancy stuff in a working-class place like this. No, the miniskirt didn't travel north of Liverpool until 1976, or thereabouts. In my experience, at least.'

Despite the circumstances, it was something of a balm to the four to actually hear about Lydia's life. It felt as though they were finally getting to know her, after all this time.

At this point Gran seemed to slip into a sort of contented reverie, but, for the others, although the sun had gone down and they were all huddled amid glinting candlelight, it had not escaped the notice of their stomachs that they had gone without dinner.

One by one, they got up and tiptoed to the kitchen to investigate what might be found.

Anne, George and Dick concentrated on the most likely cupboards around the cooker, while Julian hunted further abroad, searching for a drinks cabinet.

'Come on, I know there's a half-finished bottle of cooking sherry from 1982 around here somewhere,' they heard him muttering in the darkness.

In one corner of the kitchen, Dick discovered that quaintest of things: a pantry. As he pulled open the door, the tiny room exhaled a faintly Christmassy fragrance.

'Bound to be something in here,' he said. George and Anne gathered behind him, and looked with fascination at the tins he handed down, like archaeologists excavating a tomb.

'Corned beef, I think,' said George, turning one over in her hands.

'Just like on our old picnics!' said Anne. 'Don't know about this tin, though. There's barely any print left on the label. It looks like it went off about forty years ago.'

'Balls to that. I'm hungry. It's bound to be fine,' said George, 'as long as we have mustard to put on it. Is that mustard?'

Dick had reached up to a high shelf and brought down out of the darkness another, shallower tin. He levered off the lid, exposing a tray of white powder. They were all at a loss, but at the same time strangely impressed by the ingenuity of the wartime generation.

Dick took a spoon of powder, mixed it in a cup with water, then peered down at it through the quivering candle-light. He sniffed. '*Could* be mustard,' he said.

'Or . . . custard?' said Anne.

'Powdered egg, possibly,' suggested George.

Dick took a thoughtful sip, and cocked his head on one side. 'I think it might be hyper-long-life milk, you know,' he said.

'What are you doing with Grandad's foot powder?' said Gran, behind them.

They all screamed.

When calm had been restored, the dropped candles had been picked up and relit, and Gran was snoozing in the front room again, they heard Julian's low chuckle in the darkness.

'Quallo!' he said with deep satisfaction.

'Found a bottle of port, have you?' asked Dick.

'Not quite. Disaronno. But it'll have to do.'

'Woof,' agreed Timmy from somewhere in the gloom.

'Paws *off*,' said Julian. 'Find your bloody own!'

'*Anne, Anne,*' came a whisper. '*Anne! Wake up!*'

Anne started awake to find George's face looming over in the darkness.

'What is it?' she asked.

'Ssshhh . . .'

As her eyes adjusted, Anne saw Dick and Julian were

*One by one, they got up and tiptoed to the kitchen
to investigate what food might be found.*

both up as well, and looking concerned. She glanced at her phone and saw it was just after midnight.

Before she could ask what was going on, George gestured for her to follow and, with an elaborate pantomime, made clear they were not to disturb Gran, who was fast asleep in an armchair, snoring, with Timmy on her lap.

The four of them made a silent procession to the kitchen, where Anne judged it was safe to talk.

'What is it?' she asked.

'I thought I heard something,' George said fearfully, 'so I went outside . . .' She unlatched the back door and led them into the small garden. The almost full moon showed a discreet shed in one corner and several net-covered rows of what might have been either raspberry or gooseberry bushes.

'What is it?' Anne asked again, more testily. 'Why have you woken me up and brought me out here? It's freezing!'

But she was arrested by the solemn looks that Julian and Dick were casting towards one corner of the garden. A cloud momentarily covered the moon, and she had to move closer to make it out. Then the cloud passed, the garden was illuminated with a silvery blue light, and Anne choked back a scream.

There, in front of them, to the side of the shed, was a six-foot-long mound of freshly turfed-over earth, from the top of which stuck a spade at an almost-jaunty angle.

Anne looked round at the others, and saw the fear in their eyes too.

Through all of their minds ran a number of circumstances, all odd in themselves, which began to thread together with a sickening feeling. The decidedly suspicious proliferation of surnames Gran had accumulated throughout her life. The fact that no one in the family ever seemed to meet any of her husbands. Her secretive existence, and attempt to maintain an undocumented life. And now this ghastly final piece in the jigsaw . . .

Rather than be caught gawking at the grave by their host, who they now suspected to be a macabre murderess of the highest calibre, they all shuffled indoors, closed the door with a quiet but still agonizing squeak, and then, luring Timmy to follow them, crept upstairs to cram into their tiny bedroom again. Once inside, they fixed the door shut by moving two bookcases in front of it.

Luckily, Julian had thought to bring the bottle of Disaronno. Or, at least, he had not at any point in the proceedings, thought to put it down. They passed it round, debated in low tones what must be their next move, and, at some point in the small hours, one by one, they slipped into the land of frightened dreams.

CHAPTER FOURTEEN

The Reckoning

'Come on out!' called an angry voice. 'Come out here at once, you villains!'

Even considering the alarming discoveries of the night before, and the fitful and uneasy slumber they had enjoyed in the hours since, this was a most violent and disturbing way to be woken. Thus, four very groggy heads (not including Timmy's, as he was now practically a pro-level sleeper, and remained comatose at the end of the bed) roused themselves, blinking, to try to get to grips with this new development.

'You hear me?' the voice thundered.

'Yes, we hear you,' said Julian. 'Who the devil is this? Where's Gran?'

The door rattled. 'How *dare* you talk to me this way in my own house? Come out here! You're lucky I don't call the police!'

'I was hoping it *was* the police,' said Julian.

'I guess we get to say hello to Stan,' said Anne, dressing beneath the duvet. 'He must have come home early.'

'Ooo, rats,' said Dick.

Getting up, George quickly shoved the bookcases away from the door and found herself face to face with an elderly, but clearly very much alive, man, standing with his hands on his hips, regarding them through the reddened eyes of a high rage. They went ahead of him downstairs to the front room, where they stood next to each other, like errant schoolchildren.

'So, I'm Stan,' he said. The others introduced themselves somewhat falteringly. He shook hands with them all, not caring to conceal his ill temper.

'Now, I'd like to know, please, why, having come back three days early from my trip, I find this house practically in ruin? The electricity turned off, the phone not working, no gas . . .'

'We're terribly sorry,' said Dick. He felt that he should have followed this with a good excuse. But all he could offer was: 'We were trying to help.'

'Aye,' said Stan. Now he had set eyes on them, and realized he was merely dealing with four young nincompoops, rather than the agents of destruction he had imagined, his rage diminished a good deal. When it was established, a few minutes later, that the electricity and gas were back on, enabling him to have his first cuppa of the morning, he mellowed further. But he still had far to go before becoming anything approaching friendly. He asked them to take him through to the computer, where they showed him the different things they had tried to do, and explained the variously frustrating results.

Hearing them, he nodded once, then went to the window and thumped it open with the flat of his hand. Leaning out into the yard, he yelled, 'OZZEEEEEE!'

In the tiny room, the voice echoed awfully, and the four visitors shielded their ears. Stan went to the back door and opened it just as a red-haired child arrived, standing scarcely higher than Julian's knee. He stopped at the threshold and looked up at Stan.

'Worse than usual problems,' Stan said. 'Ice cream in it for you.'

'How muts?' asked Ozzy.

'Talk to them,' said Stan, pointing at Julian and the others.

'Literally as much ice cream as you want,' said Julian. 'Of any flavour.'

Ozzy nodded seriously and came over to the chair in front

of the computer, where he held his arms up for lifting. Anne took delight in doing so, telling him how cute his freckles were, and asking whether he knew he had a dimple, and if the pixies had given it to him, and kissing him occasionally.

But Ozzy was surprisingly indifferent to the nectar of human kindness, and instead presented a businesslike demeanour as he was placed in front of his one passion in life: the computer.

One by one, the four told him the things they had tried to do to Gran's computer ('It's *my* bloody computer,' said Stan), and what had gone wrong. Ozzy did nothing but listen and type, except for the occasional startled expression (when they revealed they had done something particularly stupid) and giggle.

After twenty minutes, during which time he had downloaded many programmes and restarted the device half a dozen times, Ozzy hopped down from the chair. He told Dick which ice cream he wanted, and Dick, clutching twenty quid of Julian's money, set off into town to procure it.

'All done,' said Ozzy.

Julian looked at him. Ozzy looked back. Julian realized it was his turn to speak.

'You are kidding,' said Julian.

Ozzy shook his head.

'Are you a witch?' Julian asked.

'No,' Ozzy said. 'I'm a pirate. Anything else?' he asked.

'I was trying to show Gran how to set up a YouTube channel, and post videos,' joked Julian. 'Wanna try that?'

Ozzy took Gran's hand as she led him into the kitchen to make him a cup of squash while they waited for Dick to return with the ice cream.

This left George, Anne, Julian and Stan grouped somewhat awkwardly in the tiny back room.

'And my wife informs me that you've deposited all her money in the bank!'

'That's right,' said Julian, with relief. At least there was one thing he could show gratitude for.

'Meaning she's seen *this*!' The banking slip trembled in Stan's hand, as he held it out. Julian took it.

'Seventy-seven thousand, three hundred quid,' Julian read, then looked back at Stan stupidly. 'What's the problem?'

'She's saved over a *quarter of a million pounds* over the years,' Stan whispered, his voice sharp as a paper cut. 'If you hadn't done this, she would never have found out that most of the notes she's saved have gone out of circulation!'

'Come on, I know there's an old bottle of cooking sherry in here somewhere,' Julian muttered.

'But . . .' George tried to protest. 'But at least this way . . .'

Anne, meanwhile, had been growing hot under the collar and perceived this was her moment to speak.

'*You* might be alive,' she said presently, to Stan. Everyone turned towards her. They had never heard a sentence that started this way, and were curious to find out where she was going with it. 'But maybe you should count yourself lucky. Look at this!'

'No, Anne!' George said. 'Please! Listen to reason! No!'

But Anne had a keen sense of justice, and there was no stopping her. She barged out into the garden, past the fruit-growing patches, and to the shed.

'Please, Anne!' said George who, having spotted tins of dog food in the pantry, felt she was beginning to see what had happened. But her words fell on deaf ears.

'Perhaps your wife – who practically gets through three husbands a decade – can explain *that* to you!' Anne pointed down at the grave victoriously.

George covered her face. Julian gawped.

Stan gasped and fell to his knees. He looked up to the sky and let out a wail that would have penetrated any heart.

94

'Snowy!' he cried, tears starting from his eyes. 'Not my precious Snowy! And I wasn't even here!'

'I was going to try to break it to him more gently than that,' Gran said quietly, from the doorway. 'But I suppose it's done now.'

They looked at each other. They looked at Stan.

When Stan's shoulders had stopped shaking and he had wiped away the tears, he nodded at them.

'Please,' he sniffed, 'I think you've done enough. We'd like some time alone . . .'

Their bags were ready in two minutes flat, and owing to the fact that their mobile reception was so terrible, and they had no number for a cab anyway, they elected to walk to the station.

Above them was a dark, overcast sky, which in no way contradicted their collective mood. When it started to spatter rain on them after a few minutes, it felt roughly justified. Arriving at the station with plenty of time to spare, and, failing to find a nearby purveyor of deep-fried food, they were forced to make do with a Gregg's.

'Well,' said Julian, as they stood on the platform, eating sausage rolls, 'we did our best. Didn't we?'

The others munched in silence. Dick looked along the tracks for a sign of their train.

'Woof,' said Timmy, trying to keep their spirits up. George tore the end of her sausage roll, and dropped it down to him.

CHAPTER FIFTEEN

Going Viral

The group found they had very little appetite for adventure in the weeks that followed. The spectre of what they had done to Granny B's finances – or, as Stan had pointed out, her awareness of them – hung over them. Whichever way they looked at it, they couldn't escape the feeling that where they had attempted to help, they had thoroughly hindered. In fact, for the first time after the conclusion of one of their adventures, they discovered they just wanted to keep their heads down and try to stay out of trouble.

So this is what they did, folding themselves into the welcoming blanket of routine: going to work, going to the gym, going to the pub, then sitting on the sofa on Sunday evenings wondering where the weekend had gone and tuning out Julian's splenetic observations on the impoverished screenwriting of whatever was on telly.

Life continued in this way for nearly a month, until, as

they lolled on the sofa one night, George, Julian and Dick were alarmed to hear Anne's voice from the kitchen area, trembling with fear.

'I think you guys should come and have a look at this . . .' she was saying.

They got up and wandered over, wondering what could possibly have unsettled her so much. She was on her laptop, and was looking at YouTube.

'Look,' she said, pointing. 'Just look.'

'It's Gran!' said Julian.

'What the flipping hell is she doing?' asked George.

On the screen in front of them was indeed visible their formerly estranged grandmother. She was pottering around in what was recognizably her kitchen, muttering to herself and (of course) making a cup of tea. She was being filmed by some device sitting on the table, almost certainly a laptop – they assumed that it was Stan who had furnished her with this, and Ozzy who had taught her how to use it.

'I don't know what it's all about,' she was saying. 'Why people make these videos and whatnot.' She broke off to let out a little chuckle as the kettle rose to the boil. 'It all seems very silly,' she said. 'I mean, this is a camera, is it?'

She leant forward to inspect the camera, and the tip of her nose ballooned to the size of an orange.

'How funny,' she said. 'Now, I'll make this for Stan, and see if he's cheered up.'

Then she straightened, and burped. 'Pardon me,' she said. And the video cut out.

The four housemates stood around the laptop, looking at the screen, wondering what they felt about it.

'It's the burp that makes it work,' said Dick.

'Makes it work?' Julian asked.

'I thought it was funny,' said George.

'I'm not talking about whether it's good,' said Dick. 'Look at the likes. Look at the *views*!'

They all gasped.

'From just one week,' said George, wonderingly.

Julian let out a single, highly offensive syllable.

'She's FAMOUS!' Anne said.

'And there are more videos, look . . .'

Dick clicked on the next video in the sidebar. This was of Gran (or 'Gramma Stubbins', as her screen name had it) talking to the camera as she tried to form a WhatsApp group for the first time. She had no idea at all what she was doing and, once the instinctive frustration that the young feel when watching older people grapple with technology wore off, it started to make them giggle. The giggle spread infectiously, and became a laugh.

And yet, whether it was through the naïvety of the production, or Gran's performance, or some other mysterious alchemy, the viewers found themselves laughing not at Gran, but most certainly with her. It was an entirely charming situation.

This second video was a week older than the previous one, and had more than three times the number of views. In the corner of the screen, at the end of each video, was a short sentence in tiny type, that explained everything: *produced by ozzy*. They looked at the comments, and then checked Twitter. Their hearts leapt into their throats, in simultaneous joy and protective dismay, as they saw that 'Gramma Stubbins' was trending.

'*What is going on?*' whispered George.

They phoned her at once.

'Her phone's working again,' said George, as she heard a ringtone. 'That's something, at least.'

Lydia answered in a lather of excitement. They showered her with congratulations. It seemed that, since it had been reconnected, her phone had been ringing off the hook. So they could all converse, George put her on speakerphone.

'And it's not just relatives and old friends,' Gran said. 'It's publishers too! I've got me a literary agent, of all things . . .'

Julian gnashed his teeth. Book publishing was, to him, a poisonous nest of halfwits, a place where the lowest of the low gathered to feast on each other's incompetence. (He had yet to forgive the dismissive tone of the rejection he had received for his historical crime novel featuring Sir Joseph Bazalgette, the Victorian engineer of the London sewers, solving murders in his spare time.) Julian scoffed, and then gasped, as George punched him in the ribs.

While it came as no surprise to Julian that YouTubers were very much the *plat du jour* for the book trade, the numbers involved were startling to them all. A smooth-talking London agent had swooped down upon Gran and, seemingly with a snap of his fingers, had auctioned off her book for a six-figure sum.

'*How* much?' Julian asked. 'Do you need a ghost writer?'

'Don't let the bugger near it!' came Stan's voice from the background.

'Thanks, love,' said Gran. 'But they've given me the lass who does Zoella. Oh!' she said. 'How's Pongo?'

Dick, still guilty over the prolific indigestion Timmy had suffered at the hands of northern cooking, opened his mouth to protest. But before he could speak Timmy let out a protesting 'Woof!'

'What's that?' asked Lydia.

'He's called Timmy,' George said. 'Not Pongo. We should have pointed that out earlier . . .'

'Oh! What was I thinking?' said Gran. 'I'll forget my own name next . . .'

'I wouldn't be at all surprised,' said Julian. 'She's had enough of them.'

Lydia sounded giddy; she sounded happy; most of all, she sounded rich. Much love was expressed in both directions over the speakerphone, after which they ended the call with the decided impression that Gran was red from beaming.

Silence reigned in the room for some moments, broken only by Timmy's gentle snoring.

'So . . .' Dick cautiously began. 'We *did*, perhaps . . .'

'You could say . . . in a rather roundabout way . . .' Julian continued. 'I mean, I *did* tell Ozzy to set Gran up with a YouTube account, after all . . . even if I was joking . . .'

George turned to Anne. 'We did help Gran. Didn't we? In the long run.'

*Anne, meanwhile, had been growing hot under the
collar at what she perceived to be an injustice.*

Anne looked from George to Dick, and then to Julian. She shrugged helplessly. 'I suppose so, despite our best efforts,' she said. 'If it will help you sleep.'

They all flopped into chairs around the kitchen table. It was a wonderful relief.

'So she'll really be financially safe, after all,' said Dick. 'And can enjoy her retirement.'

'There's one pensioner who I'm not going to allow to rest,' said George, pointing at the dog curled up asleep on the sofa. 'We're not putting you out to pasture yet, Timmy. Get your arse over here. Until you get over this bout of sleeping sickness, I'm going to walk your bloody legs off, young man!'

'Woof,' said Timmy groggily, rousing himself and then, shaking the sleep from his head, bounding over to her. 'Woof!'